THAT'S WHAT HAPPENS
When It's <u>Spring!</u>

by Elaine W. Good
Illustrated by Susie Shenk

Good Books

Intercourse, Pennsylvania 17534

C.I.P. data may be found on page 32
Copyright © 1987 by Good Books, Intercourse, PA 17534

Today I wonder, "When is it spring?" Mommy takes my hand. "Come, I'll show you." Out in the flower bed tiny green knobs are peeping out of the ground. "That will be a tulip and this a crocus!" Mommy says.

That's what happens when it's spring!

Daddy and I find little green things pushing up through the brown grass in the yard. "Daffodils!" Daddy tells me.

That's what happens when it's spring!

We go to the meadow to check the willow trees we planted last summer. They look all brown and dead. Then I spot a baby green leaf on one branch. And another! And another! Oh, they are alive!

That's what happens when it's spring!

My neighbor, Betsy, and I ride my tricycle. We take turns coasting down the barn hill. It feels good to play outside.

That's what happens when it's spring!

My sister, Caroline, sees skunk cabbage flowers in the meadow on her way home from school.

That's what happens when it's spring!

Daddy plows the garden. I dig in it with Michael. We use his backhoe and my
skid loader and dump trunk. We get all dirty.

That's what happens when it's spring!

Daddy and I take away the mulch we had put over the rhubarb last fall. Lots and lots of teeny red bumps are coming up.

That's what happens when it's spring!

Tonight after his evening chores my brother, David, and I go fishing. I hold the rod a long time but nothing happens, so I give it back to David. Just as I walk away he yells, "I got one!" He hands the rod to me again and I carefully reel in a rainbow trout!

That's what happens when it's spring!

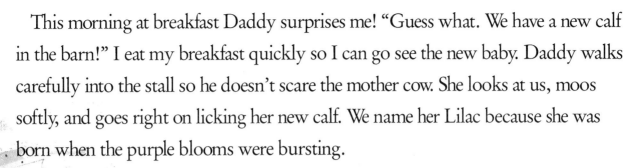

This morning at breakfast Daddy surprises me! "Guess what. We have a new calf in the barn!" I eat my breakfast quickly so I can go see the new baby. Daddy walks carefully into the stall so he doesn't scare the mother cow. She looks at us, moos softly, and goes right on licking her new calf. We name her Lilac because she was born when the purple blooms were bursting.

That's what happens when it's spring!

Michael and I dig in the warm soft dirt under the swings. Then Mommy calls me
for a story at naptime. "Look at your dirty pants!" she says. "Let's take them off."
That's what happens when it's spring!

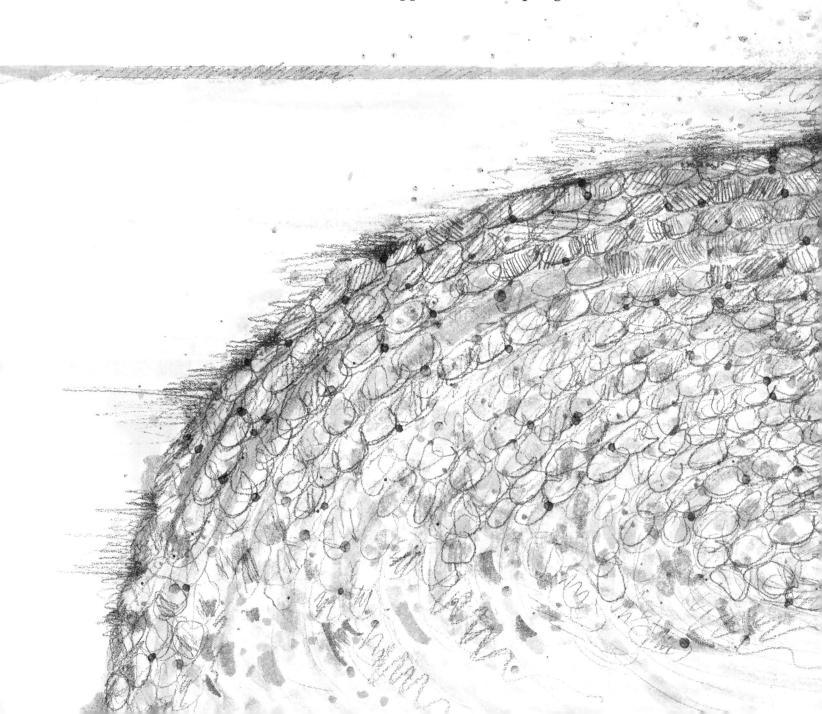

On the day before Easter Mommy cooks some eggs and we all help paint them.

That's what happens when it's spring!

Our family goes for a walk in the woods. We hunt wild flowers—spring beauty, trout lilies, henbit and violets. My sister, Christine, surprises a frog at the edge of a little pool.

That's what happens when it's spring!

After my nap this afternoon Mommy and I walk through the meadow. Mommy has a dishpan and a knife so she can cut dandelion plants. "We will eat these for supper," she says when I spy a thin wavy leaf. I taste it. I decide I would rather pick dandelion flowers.

That's what happens when it's spring!

Yesterday, I was planting corn under our big maple tree. When I went into the house for my disc, Mommy said, "You look hot. Let's take off your sweatshirt." This morning I went outside without my sweatshirt, but soon I came back. Today I want my jacket! The wind is cold! Funny thing though, the sun just came out, and now I'm hot again.

That's what happens when it's spring!

Today I wonder, when will summer come? "After Daddy's birthday and after David, Caroline, and Christine are out of school," Mommy smiles. I can't wait! I love summer!

What will happen when it's summer?

That's What Happens When It's Spring!
Copyright © 1987 by Good Books, Intercourse, PA 17534

International Standard Book Number: 0-934672-53-9
Library of Congress Catalog Card Number: 87-14964

Library of Congress Cataloging-in-Publication Data

Good, Elaine W., 1944–
    That's what happens when it's spring!

    Summary: A rural child discovers the sights, sounds, colors, and special feeling of spring.
    |1. Spring—Fiction. 2. Country life—Fiction|

I. Shenk, Susie, 1956–   ill.   II. Title.
PZ7.G5996Th 1987 |E| 87-14964
ISBN 0-934672-53-9

MONTE VISTA CHRISTIAN CHURCH
3501 Campus Blvd., N. E.
Albuquerque, New Mexico